Here are some other Redfeather Books you will enjoy

The Curse of the Trouble Dolls
by Dian Curtis Regan

Max Malone the Magnificent
by Charlotte Herman

A Moon in Your Lunch Box
by Michael Spooner

The Peppermint Race
by Dian Curtis Regan

The Riddle Streak
by Susan Beth Pfeffer

Sable
by Karen Hesse

Sara Kate, Superkid
by Susan Beth Pfeffer

Snakes Are Nothing to Sneeze At
by Gabrielle Charbonnet

Tutu Much Ballet
by Gabrielle Charbonnet

Twin Surprises
by Susan Beth Pfeffer

Twin Troubles
by Susan Beth Pfeffer

Weird Wolf
by Margery Cuyler

Available in paperback

SARA KATE Saves the World

Susan Beth Pfeffer

illustrated by

Tony DeLuna

A REDFEATHER BOOK

Henry Holt and Company · *New York*

For Beth Denninger,
who probably could save the world
—S. B. P.

Henry Holt and Company, Inc.
Publishers since 1866
115 West 18th Street
New York, New York 10011

Henry Holt is a registered trademark
of Henry Holt and Company, Inc.
Text copyright © 1995 by Susan Beth Pfeffer
Illustrations copyright © 1995 by Tony DeLuna. All rights reserved.
Published in Canada by Fitzhenry & Whiteside Ltd.,
195 Allstate Parkway, Markham, Ontario L3R 4T8.

Library of Congress Cataloging-in-Publication Data
Pfeffer, Susan Beth. Sara Kate saves the world /
Susan Beth Pfeffer; illustrated by Tony DeLuna.
p.   cm.—(A Redfeather Book)
Summary: Sara Kate is disappointed that her superpowers
aren't more heroic, until she uses her X-ray vision to
make the school bully leave her alone.
[1. Supernatural—Fiction.   2. Schools—
Fiction.   3. Bullies—Fiction.]   I. DeLuna, Tony, ill.
II. Title.   III. Series: Redfeather Books.
PZ7.P44855Sak   1995   [Fic]—dc20   94-41628

ISBN 0-8050-3148-0
First Edition—1995
Printed in the United States of America on acid-free paper.∞

1 3 5 7 9 10 8 6 4 2

Contents

SARA KATE
Saves the World

1

Higher and Higher

"Look, Stevie! Look at what I can do!" Sara Kate called to her older brother.

"I'm looking," Stevie said with a sigh.

"Then say something!" Sara Kate said. "Isn't it great, how high I can jump?"

"So you can jump to the top of a tree," Stevie said. "Big deal. All you're doing is scaring squirrels."

"I am not," Sara Kate said. "The squirrels like it when I keep them company. They like making new friends."

"Then how come they keep running away?"

Stevie asked. And sure enough, two squirrels ran out of the tree just as Sara Kate was touching the highest branch.

"They want to tell their friends about me," Sara Kate said as soon as she touched ground. "You're just jealous."

"I am not," Stevie said.

"Are too," Sara Kate said. "You've been jealous of me ever since I got superpowers and you didn't."

"They're dumb superpowers," Stevie said. "Jumping like that. It doesn't get you anything to be able to jump high."

"Remember my first superpower?" Sara Kate asked.

"Yeah, I remember," Stevie said. "It was only last month. You don't need superpowers to remember a month ago."

"I could throw basketballs and they'd all go in the basket," Sara Kate said. "It didn't matter where I threw them from. That was a great superpower. And I almost won a thousand dollars from it."

"You *didn't*," Stevie pointed out. "All you got out of it was a teddy bear."

"But he's my favorite teddy bear," Sara Kate said. "Watch me, Stevie. I'm going to jump even higher now."

Stevie yawned. Sara Kate jumped. It felt like flying, she went so high in the air. She could look down on the trees. Even Stevie looked small.

And when she came down, she landed lightly on her feet. She didn't even scuff her shoes. "I bet I'm the best jumper ever," she said.

"Big deal," Stevie said. "For one day you could throw baskets. Today you can jump. I'm real impressed."

"I've had other superpowers," Sara Kate said. "Like last Saturday."

"That's right," Stevie said. "Last Saturday you could hold your breath for twenty minutes. I liked that one. At least you kept your mouth shut for a while."

"You can't hold your breath for twenty minutes," Sara Kate said. "You can't throw a basket-

6

ball from miles away and have it go in the basket."

"Neither can you," Stevie said. "All you can do today is jump. And pretty soon you won't even be able to do that."

Sara Kate knew Stevie was right, but she wasn't ready to listen to him. So she jumped again. This time she bounded high enough to touch the roof of her house.

"You'd better watch it," Stevie said. "Mom's taking a nap. You might wake her."

"Then she'll have to believe I have superpowers," Sara Kate said.

"She'll just think you're weird," Stevie said. "Like I do."

Sara Kate sighed. She loved having superpowers, but there were a lot of problems. Her parents refused to believe she had them, and Stevie was jealous, and after a while even something like jumping so high you could touch the roof of your house got boring. She'd never admit it to Stevie, but holding her breath for twenty minutes had practically driven her crazy because it meant she couldn't talk.

She had liked throwing baskets, though. That had been when she'd found out she had superpowers. Gran had explained it all to her. Some of the girls in her family were born with them. And if you were lucky enough to be one of them, the superpowers would hit on Tuesdays and Thursdays and sometimes on Saturdays. There was no way of knowing which superpower you'd get that day, or if you'd get one at all. Your arm got tingly, sort of like it was asleep, and then there'd be a superpower, and then after a few hours your arm would get tingly again, and the superpower would go away.

Now that Sara Kate thought about it, her arm was feeling kind of tingly. Soon she wouldn't be able to jump high.

"One more," she said to Stevie. "And then I'm quitting."

But Stevie had already gone inside. Sara Kate sighed, and then jumped. She jumped so high she thought she could touch the clouds.

But all she touched was air. She floated down to the ground, felt her arm tingle some more, and began to wonder just what good super-powers were anyway.

2

The New Girl
and the
Old Bully

Sara Kate had found she liked school more on Mondays, Wednesdays, and Fridays ever since she'd discovered her superpowers. On Tuesdays and Thursdays she kept waiting for her arm to tingle, and it was hard to pay attention to the teacher.

She got to school early on Monday. She was looking forward to the day's lessons. In science they were going to study worms. Sara Kate wanted to learn if it was true that when you cut one in half, both parts lived. Stevie said that happened, but Stevie made stuff up sometimes. Once

10

he'd said if he cut Sara Kate in half, both parts of her would live. Sara Kate knew that was a lie, but that was before she had superpowers. Now maybe it was true (but she wasn't about to find out).

There were lots of kids in the playground, waiting for the school bell to ring. Sara Kate was walking over to a couple of her friends when she saw a girl standing all by herself near the door.

The girl was new. Sara Kate could tell right away. The girl looked scared and alone, and she was dressed much too nice for normal.

Sara Kate thought about going on to her friends, but decided to say hello to the new girl. She walked over to the door and smiled.

"My name is Sara Kate," she said. "Are you new here?"

The girl nodded. "My name is Ashley," she said. "We just moved into our new house, so I'm starting school here late."

"I'm in third grade," Sara Kate said.

"Me too," Ashley said. "Maybe we'll be in the same class."

11

"That'd be nice," Sara Kate said. She tried to think of something else to say to Ashley, but all she could think of were her superpowers, and she didn't like to brag about them. "Do you have any brothers or sisters?" she asked instead.

"I have a little sister," Ashley said. "She's fun, but I wish I had a big brother."

"I have a big brother," Sara Kate said. "Little sisters are lots more fun."

The two girls giggled. Sara Kate decided she liked Ashley.

"Hello, stupids."

Sara Kate looked around and saw Dicky Logan walking toward them. Dicky was the biggest, meanest boy in her class. "Go away, Dicky," she said.

"I will not," he said. "It's a free country. I can stand here and look at stupid, ugly girls as much as I want."

Ashley looked like she was about to cry. Sara Kate felt bad for her. She didn't want Ashley to think that all the kids at her school were like Dicky.

"Don't pay any attention to him," she said to

12

Ashley. "That's just Dicky Logan. He's the worst kid in this school."

Dicky moved right next to Sara Kate and looked down at her. "What did you call me?" he asked.

"I didn't call you anything," Sara Kate said.

"You said I was the worst," Dicky said. "Didn't you, Stupid Face."

Why did it have to be a Monday? If Sara Kate still had her Saturday superpower, she could have jumped right over Dicky. Instead she was stuck standing next to him, feeling smaller and smaller.

"I didn't say worst," Sara Kate lied. "I said first. I meant you were the first one in every day, and you were the first one whenever we had races." *And the first to get into trouble*, she thought.

"That's better, Ugly Face," Dicky said. "But you'd better watch what you say around me. You too, Double Ugly." He made a face at the girls and then walked off.

"You said worst, not first," Ashley said to Sara Kate.

14

Sara Kate nodded. "I'm sorry I lied," she said.

"I can never think of things to say when I get in trouble like that," Ashley said. "You must be really smart."

"Or really scared," Sara Kate said, and the two girls giggled together again. But Sara Kate couldn't help thinking about her superpowers and how she wished she could use them for something worthwhile.

3
How to be
a Hero

Sara Kate was helping her mother make a salad for supper that night. Her mother cut the vegetables while Sara Kate tore the lettuce into little pieces. That was her favorite job in the world.

"What's the best thing you ever did, Mommy?" she asked her mother.

"Marrying your father and having you and Stevie," her mother replied.

That was a nice answer, but it wasn't what Sara Kate was looking for. "I mean besides that," Sara Kate said. "I mean what was the best thing you ever did for the world?"

16

"You mean like recycling?" her mother asked.

That wasn't it either, Sara Kate thought. "I mean did you ever save anybody's life?" she asked. "Or maybe somebody was getting robbed, and you captured the crook. Or a house was on fire, and you put it out all by yourself. Something like that."

Sara Kate's mother put down her knife for a moment and thought. "I don't think I ever did anything like that," she said. "Most people don't. Most people think it's enough to raise a family and recycle."

"Oh," Sara Kate said.

"Why do you ask?" her mother said. She started slicing a cucumber again. "Do you want to be a hero?"

Sara Kate hadn't put a word to it before, but that was it, all right. She wanted to be a hero. Why else have superpowers if not to save the world? "Yes," she said. "That's just what I want to be."

"That's a very good ambition," her mother said.

"But there are lots of different ways of being a hero."

"Like what?" Sara Kate asked. "Besides rescuing people."

"Well, some people think teachers are heroes," her mother said. "And police officers and firefighters certainly are. They rescue people. You could be any of those things."

"Don't you have to be a grown-up?" Sara Kate asked.

"Oh," her mother said. "I didn't realize you wanted to be a hero right away."

Sara Kate knew she was going to have her superpowers for the rest of her life, and she was sure someday they'd be a big help if she decided to become a police officer or a firefighter. But she didn't see why she had to wait so long if she had the superpowers already. "I do," Sara Kate said. "What kind of a hero can I be this week?"

"That's a hard one," her mother said. "I think you'd be a hero if you did your schoolwork and cleaned your room and helped with your chores and got into fewer fights with Stevie. But you want more than that, don't you?"

"That's not real hero stuff," Sara Kate said. "I want to be the kind of hero that's on TV."

"Any reason why?" her mother asked. "Did something happen at school today that made you decide you wanted to be a hero right now?"

Sara Kate decided it was easier to talk about Dicky than to explain about her superpowers again. "There was this new girl named Ashley," she said. "She's in my class and she seems really nice, and Dicky Logan walked up to us and picked on us for no reason. And it was a Monday, so there was nothing I could do about it."

"You mean on Friday maybe you could have done something because he'd have the whole weekend to forget?" Sara Kate's mother said. That wasn't at all what Sara Kate meant, but there was no point telling her mother anything else.

"He made me feel bad," Sara Kate said. "He's so mean."

"He is," her mother said. "I spoke to your teacher last year about Dicky. They're trying to get help for him, so maybe he'll learn he doesn't have to be mean all the time."

"What if he doesn't get help?" Sara Kate asked. "What if I did something to him to make him stop being so bad?"

"Like what?" her mother asked.

Sara Kate wasn't sure. Leaping over him had seemed like a good idea this morning, but now that she thought about it, that didn't seem like enough to stop Dicky. "I don't know," she said. "But I bet there's something I could do."

"You could try being nice to him," Sara Kate's mother said. "That would be a really heroic thing, making friends with a boy who has that many problems."

Sara Kate sighed. She didn't think even on a Tuesday or Thursday her superpowers were strong enough to make her be nice to Dicky Logan.

She'd just have to think of some other way to be a hero.

4
The World's Strongest Superkid

Sara Kate woke up on Tuesday with her arm tingling like crazy. *This is it*, she thought. *This is going to be the superpower that will help me save the world.*

"You're in a good mood this morning," her mother said. "Did you work out a way of dealing with Dicky?"

Sara Kate hadn't even thought about Dicky. It depended what her superpower was going to be, she realized. "I just woke up happy," she said.

"That's nice," her mother said. "We should all wake up happy more often. That's one way we could make the world a better place."

Sara Kate felt the most awful urge to pick up the refrigerator and toss it around. But there was no way she could do that without her mother noticing.

"I forgot something in my room," she said. "Bye, Mom. I'll be back for breakfast in a minute."

"Bye, honey," her mother said, giving her a funny look. Sara Kate didn't care. She raced up the stairs and closed the door to her bedroom. She then picked up the chest of drawers with her right hand. With her left hand, she scratched her nose.

"I'm the strongest person in the world," she whispered. This was too good to keep to herself. She put down the chest as quietly as possible and ran into Stevie's bedroom.

"See how strong I am!" she shouted as she picked up his desk and twirled it around her head.

"So now you're strong," Stevie said. "Big deal."

"It is a big deal," Sara Kate said. "It's a great superpower. I can do wonderful things being strong."

"Like what?" Stevie asked.

Sara Kate knew there were a thousand wonderful things she could do if she could just think of them. "I can lift things," she said.

"I can see that," Stevie said. "But what are you going to lift? Desks?"

"I can lift people," Sara Kate said.

"Don't think about lifting me," Stevie said. "You may be the strongest person in the world today, but tomorrow I'll be stronger than you again."

"I wasn't going to lift you," Sara Kate said, but now that Stevie had mentioned it, it did seem like a fun thing to do. She pictured picking him up and twirling him around, and giggled.

"Don't even think about it," Stevie said.

"Would it scare you?" Sara Kate asked. "Not if I picked you up, but if somebody else did."

"I guess," Stevie said. "What? You're going to rent your superpowers to other people?"

"I don't think I can," Sara Kate said, but she'd figured out what she could do with her strength to make the world a better place. "I love you, Stevie," she said. "You're the best big brother ever."

"Just don't kiss me," Stevie said.

Sara Kate didn't plan to. Instead she ran downstairs and ate her breakfast in record time.

"I have to go to school now," she said. "Bye, Mom. Bye, Dad."

"Isn't it awfully early?" her father asked.

"I'm meeting some kids," Sara Kate said. "See you later."

"Don't forget your schoolbooks," her mother said.

Sara Kate grinned. She almost had forgotten them in her rush. She picked them up and tried to act like they were heavy. But as soon as she left her house, she began carrying them with just two fingers high above her head. She really only needed one finger, but she had better balance with two.

Her plan was simple, and it was bound to work. She'd get to school, find Dicky, and pick him up.

After she'd spun him around a few times, he'd be sure to behave himself. Of course she'd have to do it where nobody else could see them or else she'd have a lot of explaining to do. And then no one would know it was because of Sara Kate that Dicky had reformed. But she'd still be a hero, at least to herself.

She raced to the schoolyard and looked around. There was no Dicky. As her friends arrived they asked her to join them, on the swings, on the ropes, playing tag. But Sara Kate stood by herself, watching and waiting.

She stood that way until the bell rang. And then she sighed. Her great plan was missing just one thing—Dicky.

5

Let's Pretend
to Fly

Sara Kate couldn't remember a worse day at school.

Every time she heard a sound, she turned around to see if Dicky had come in. Of course he hadn't. Dicky missed a lot of school, and this was just another one of those days he didn't show up.

What made things worse was Sara Kate's constant wish to lift things. She knew she'd get in trouble if she just started picking up desks, bookshelves, or other kids, the way she wanted to. She never knew how hard it was to pretend to be weak. And it was really hard to pay attention to her lessons when all she wanted to do was lift the teachers up over her head and twirl them around for a while.

Finally the long school day ended. Sara Kate grabbed her books, taking care to carry them the ordinary way, and ran outdoors. If she didn't find something to lift, she'd go crazy.

She walked a few blocks from the school to Oak Street. There were lots of houses there, and plenty of parked cars, but she didn't see any people.

Sara Kate walked over to one of the cars. She put her books down, bent her knees, and lifted the car.

It was heavier than it looked. Sara Kate needed both her arms to get the car off the ground, and she didn't think she'd be able to lift it over her head. Once she'd raised it about three feet, she put it down carefully. No one came out of the houses to ask how she'd done it. Sara Kate wasn't sure whether she was relieved or disappointed.

29

There had to be something she could lift that would make the world a better place, she thought. Maybe not a car or a person, but something.

Sara Kate tried to figure out what that might be. Then she imagined a person being crushed by something really heavy. A rock, maybe. A giant rock falls on someone, and it's too heavy for anybody else to lift. But a big rock would be nothing for her. At least not today.

Sara Kate walked over to the town park. That was as likely a place to find somebody being crushed by a rock as anywhere else in town. But all she saw were kids playing and some grownups sitting on benches, watching. Nobody needed to have anything lifted off them.

"Hi, Sara Kate."

"Oh, hi, Ashley," Sara Kate said.

"My mother sent me to the park," Ashley said. "She's still unpacking and she wanted me out of the way."

"Oh," Sara Kate said. Maybe Ashley's mother

could use some help moving furniture. "Do you have a piano?" she asked.

"No," Ashley said. "I play the violin, though."

Sara Kate shook her head. There was no trick to lifting a violin.

"Do you want to play something?" Ashley asked. "Or go on the swings?"

"I don't think so," Sara Kate said. It was hard to explain that what she really wanted to do was lift the swings. "Maybe tomorrow. I feel kind of weird today." She did feel weird, too. It took her a moment to realize her arm was tingling. In a few minutes she wouldn't be strong anymore, and she hadn't done anything wonderful.

"Could somebody help me?" a woman called. "I can't get out of my parking space because of this motorcycle blocking my path."

Sara Kate ran over to the woman to see if she could help. But by the time she got there, her arm was no longer tingling. She sighed. Two men came over and hauled the motorcycle away from the woman's car.

Sara Kate walked back to Ashley. "Let's go on the swings," she said. "I feel like doing that now."

"Good," Ashley said. "Swings are my favorite. They always make me feel like I'm flying."

Sara Kate nodded. She hadn't had flying as a superpower, but with her luck, she'd get it when she was locked in the bathroom. She giggled at the thought.

"What's so funny?" Ashley asked as the girls climbed on the swings.

"Nothing," Sara Kate said. "I was just thinking it would be fun to be able to fly."

"Or to be really strong," Ashley said. "Sometimes I wish I was so strong, I could lift anything. Like that motorcycle."

"Nobody's that strong," Sara Kate said. "Come on. Let's pretend to fly."

6

What's the Point of Superpowers?

"So I thought I could pick him up," Sara Kate said to her grandmother the next afternoon. "And spin him around and scare him. And then he'd be nicer, at least to me and my friends. Because I'd scare him by being so strong."

"That sounds like a good plan," Gran said. "Did it work?"

"He wasn't in school," Sara Kate said. "I never had the chance."

"What a shame," Gran said. "Come on. Let's have some milk and cookies while we talk."

Sara Kate followed Gran into her kitchen. "What

superpower did you have yesterday?" she asked.

"Well, yesterday I felt like doing jumping jacks," Gran said, "and once I got started, there was no stopping me. I must have jumped for three hours straight. So I treated myself to cookies. Have one. They're really good."

Sara Kate took a cookie. Gran was right. They were delicious. "What's the point of having superpowers if you can't do stuff with them?" she asked. "All I got out of being so strong was lifting a car when nobody could see me. That didn't help anybody."

"Oh dear," Gran said. "I hope you don't think there's any point in having superpowers."

"There isn't any point at all?" Sara Kate asked, and took a big gulp of milk.

"None that I can think of," Gran said. "It's like having blue eyes. There's no point to it. It's just the way your body turned out."

"I have brown eyes," Sara Kate said.

"Brown eyes, then," Gran said. "Saturday you jumped. Tuesday you lifted cars. That's all."

"But I should have been able to think of something to do when I was so strong to help people," Sara Kate said. "If I'd scared Dicky, that would have helped. Or I could have lifted the motorcycle. Or I could have jumped up and rescued a kitten or something. Or I could have saved someone who was drowning when I could hold my breath. But I never seem to have a power when I can use it for something."

"That's just the way it is with superpowers," Gran said. "You can never count on them. I remember once, I was just about your age, and I bragged to everybody I could beat them in a race. My arm was tingly and I just felt so fast. So of course they all agreed to race against me, and it turned out my superpower had nothing to do with being fast. It was bending. Everybody was running fast as can be, and I was twisting my body in a thousand different shapes. And all my friends thought that was weird. I didn't get to be fast until I was thirty-seven years old."

"Did you do anything good when you were strong?" Sara Kate asked.

Gran thought about it. "Once," she said. "I was in a cemetery and I saw one of the tombstones had been knocked down. I picked it up and put it where it belonged. But that's about all."

"Why were you in a cemetery?" Sara Kate asked.

"You know, I have no idea," Gran said. "I'm sure I had a perfectly good reason, but whatever it was, I've forgotten it. I wish I could get my superpowers to improve my memory."

"I miss being able to throw basketballs," Sara Kate said.

"I know," Gran said, patting Sara Kate on her head. "That looked like a wonderful superpower. Lots of fun and no responsibilities. The best kind."

"I liked jumping high, too," Sara Kate said. "And lifting the car was kind of fun. Holding my breath wasn't so great, but all my other superpowers have been fun. I just want to do good with them."

"Maybe you will one day," Gran said. "Maybe

not the way you think you will, but something good might come out of them. Take me. I did three hours' worth of jumping jacks, and I got to eat these cookies. Now that's what I call a really useful superpower!"

7

ELBUORT Is Trouble Spelled Backwards

It had been a very nice Saturday, even nicer, Sara Kate realized, because she hadn't had any superpowers to deal with. She never thought she'd enjoy a day off from them, but this Saturday she was happy none had shown up.

She'd spent the afternoon with Ashley. Sara Kate liked having a new friend. She and Ashley had played in Sara Kate's attic for a while. Then they went to the park and played there. They'd run into some of Sara Kate's other friends, and they all had had a good time together on the playground equipment.

Both girls were due home before supper. They left their friends in the park and began the walk home. Ashley's house was on the way to Sara Kate's, so they got to walk home almost all the way together.

They were on Maple Street when Sara Kate first felt her arm starting to tingle. *Oh no,* she thought. How could she explain it to Ashley if she suddenly felt the urge to fly?

"I like Mr. Daley," Ashley was saying. "But I don't like memorizing my times tables."

SELBAT, Sara Kate thought. *Tables* spelled backward.

She couldn't believe it. Her new superpower was the ability to spell words backward.

"How do you do it?" Ashley asked. "Do you just look at them or does someone in your family help you memorize?"

EZIROMEM. Sara Kate shook her head, trying to get the letters out of her mind.

"Neither?" Ashley asked. "Then how do you learn them?"

MEHT. Sara Kate was spared trying to answer by the cries of a woman. "Help me! Help me! I've fallen and hurt myself!"

FLESYM, Sara Kate thought, but she and Ashley both ran to where the woman was lying. She was on the sidewalk, with all her groceries scattered around her.

"I think I broke my ankle," the woman said. "Please girls, get me some help!"

PLEH, Sara Kate thought. She couldn't believe it. Here was a woman who needed rescuing and Sara Kate wasn't strong enough to carry her to the hospital, the way she could have just a few days earlier. All she could do was spell *help* backward. What kind of superpower was that?

"What should we do?" Ashley asked.

OD, Sara Kate thought. "Ashley, you stay with her," she said. "I'll knock on doors until I find somebody home."

"Okay," Ashley said.

YAKO, Sara Kate said to herself. She watched as Ashley began gathering the cans and boxes

42

that had scattered on the sidewalk, and then she ran to the nearest house and knocked. When there was no answer, she tried the next house and the next, until finally a man opened his door.

"What do you want, little girl?" the man asked.

LRIG. Life really would be much easier if nobody talked to her, Sara Kate thought. "There's a lady on the street," she said, pointing at her. "She fell and she thinks she broke her ankle."

"I'll call for an ambulance," the man said. "You go back there and tell her help is on the way."

YAW. "Thank you," Sara Kate said. She ran back to the woman and relayed the message. Sure enough, in just a few minutes there was an ambulance.

"Thank you so much," the woman said to Sara Kate and Ashley. "I don't know what I would have done without you."

Sara Kate and Ashley said "You're welcome," but Sara Kate couldn't stop thinking how much more exciting things would have been if she'd had the right superpower at the right time.

Her arm began tingling again, and Sara Kate felt nothing but relief when she lost her ability to spell words backward. *What a totally useless superpower*, she thought—not that any of her superpowers seemed much better.

"That was so exciting," Ashley said as they reached her home. "I thought you were great, the way you figured out what to do."

"You were a big help too," Sara Kate said. "Picking up the lady's groceries and all that."

"I guess we make a good team," Ashley said.

"I guess so too," Sara Kate said. But then she felt truly awful. Real superheroes didn't need teams. They could save the world all alone, with the help of their trusty superpowers.

None of which involved spelling words backward.

8
Double Hard to be a Hero

As soon as Sara Kate got home, she went to her bedroom and began crying. It just wasn't fair. All she wanted to do was help people, and nothing seemed to work. And now she'd had the worst, most useless superpower of all. Spelling words backward. If she had a spelling test, spelling words forward would come in handy, but backward? All it did was give her a headache.

"Sara Kate? Are you okay?"

Sara Kate stopped sniffling long enough to see Stevie at her bedroom door.

"I heard you crying," he said. "Did something

46

bad happen? Did Dicky bother you or something?"

"No," Sara Kate said, but then she really started bawling. Stevie entered her room and found her box of tissues, which he plopped next to her.

"What happened?" he asked. "Did someone hurt you?"

"No," Sara Kate sobbed. "It's my superpowers."

"Did you lose them, maybe?" Stevie asked. Sara Kate couldn't help noticing how hopeful Stevie sounded.

"I still have them," she said. She took a tissue and blew her nose. "Only they keep getting stupider."

"They were never very bright," Stevie said.

Sara Kate started crying again.

"I'm sorry," Stevie said, and he looked like he really was, too. "What happened this time?"

"I was having this really nice day, and then my arm started tingling and the next thing I knew I could spell words backward," Sara Kate said.

Stevie stared at her for a moment, and then

he began laughing. "Backward?" he said. "Can you still do it?"

Sara Kate shook her head. "It only lasted for a few minutes," she said. "And there was this woman on the sidewalk. She fell and broke her ankle, and all I could do was spell words backward. Did you know *help* is PLEH?"

"I never really thought about it," Stevie said. "What happened to the woman?"

"Oh, I told Ashley—she's my new friend I told you about—anyway, I told her to stay with the lady, and I knocked on people's doors until I found somebody to call an ambulance," Sara Kate said. "And it was so hard because every time anyone said something to me, I spelled the word backward in my head. Superman never did that."

"I don't think so," Stevie said. "But I don't think he could have done much better than you did."

"Sure, he could have," Sara Kate said. "He would have lifted the lady up and flown her to the hospital. She wouldn't have needed an ambulance."

"But even if you'd had a real superpower, you couldn't have done that," Stevie said. "If you had been strong enough to carry her, you couldn't have flown. And if you had been able to fly, you wouldn't have had the strength to carry her. Your superpowers don't work that way."

"They don't work at all," Sara Kate grumbled.

"I think what you did was much better than superpowers," Stevie said. "You saw somebody in trouble and you figured out what to do to help her. And it was double hard for you because you kept spelling *help* backward."

"Not just *help*," Sara Kate said, and then in spite of herself she giggled. "I was afraid somebody was going to end a sentence with *ambulance*," she said. "I didn't know how I was going to spell it backward, because I don't know how to spell it frontward yet."

Stevie laughed. "You should be proud of yourself," he said. "A lot of little kids wouldn't have known what to do. They would have just stood there or even run away. Have you told Mom and Dad yet?"

"Not yet," Sara Kate said. "Do you think I should?"

"Of course," Stevie said. "I'd leave out the part about spelling words backward, though. They'll like it better that way."

"All right," Sara Kate said. "Thank you, Stevie."

"You're welcome, I guess," Stevie said. "And thank you, Sara Kate."

"For what?" Sara Kate asked.

"For making me so happy I don't have stupid superpowers," he said. "That's *SREWOPREPUS*, in case you were wondering."

Sara Kate tossed her pillow at him, but she didn't mind when she missed him. She had done something good that day. The only problem was it was *in spite of* instead of *because of* her superpowers.

9
Superpowers
and
Teddy Bears

At recess on Tuesday, Sara Kate and Ashley were playing in the schoolyard. Dicky walked over to them.

"How are Stupid Face and Ugly Breath?" he asked.

"Go away, Dicky," Sara Kate said.

"You heard her," Ashley said. "Go away, Dicky."

"It's a free country," Dicky said. "I can stand here as long as I want. Of course, looking at the two of you makes me want to puke."

"Then puke someplace else," Ashley said.

52

Sara Kate didn't say anything. Her arm was tingling. *This is it*, she thought. Finally she was going to have a superpower when she needed it. And it wasn't going to be spelling words backward. She never had the same superpower twice in a row.

"You look funny," Dicky said. "Stupider than ever."

Sara Kate shook her head. It wasn't just her arm that felt funny. She closed her eyes for a moment, and when she opened them, everybody around her looked strange.

Then she realized why. She could see right through everyone's clothes to their underwear!

Sara Kate couldn't help it. She began to laugh. She'd never seen anything so silly as the sight of her entire class in different kinds of underwear.

"What are you laughing at?" Dicky asked. "Are you laughing at me?"

Sara Kate turned around to face him and began laughing even harder. Dicky, the meanest boy in the world, had teddy bear underwear on.

"You *are* laughing at me," Dicky said.

"No, I'm not," Sara Kate said. "Honest." But she kept laughing.

"Stop that," Dicky said. "Or I'll bash your head in."

"Right," Sara Kate said. "You and what teddy bear?" She was laughing so hard, she thought she'd die.

"Teddy bear?" Dicky asked. "What do you mean by that?"

Sara Kate could see Dicky was really upset. Ashley was curious about what was happening. She had on all-white underwear. Sara Kate sure hoped her arm would start tingling again real soon.

"I said, what do you mean by teddy bear?" Dicky asked.

Sara Kate bit down on her lip hard to stop her laughter. "Let's talk," she said to Dicky. "In private."

"Sara Kate," Ashley said, but Sara Kate just shook her head. She grabbed Dicky by the arm and led him to a tree where no one else was nearby.

"You have teddy bear underwear on," Sara Kate whispered to him. "That's why I was laughing."

"I do not!" Dicky shouted.

"You do too," Sara Kate said. "I can tell."

"You're crazy," Dicky said.

"I am not," Sara Kate said. "They're blue and the teddy bears are brown and they have sweet little smiles on their faces. And your undershirt is a little torn."

Dicky turned pale. "How do you know that?" he asked.

"I know lots of stuff," Sara Kate said. What she knew was the color of everybody's underwear in her class that day, but there was no point telling Dicky that.

"Like what?" Dicky asked. "Did my mom tell you what kind of underwear I'd have on?"

"Of course not," Sara Kate said. "Whose mom would tell people that?"

56

"I don't know," Dicky said. "But how else could you know?"

"I have ways," Sara Kate said. "You might even say I have superpowers. Now if you'll excuse me, Teddy. I mean Dicky." She giggled some more.

"You're not going to tell anybody, are you?" Dicky asked. "My grandma gave them to me, and my mom says I have to wear them until I outgrow them."

"I can tell if I want to," Sara Kate said. "It's a free country. And you've been awfully mean to me, Dicky. Why should I be nice to you?"

"I won't be mean to you ever again," Dicky said. "I promise. Just don't tell anybody."

"You can't be mean to Ashley either," Sara Kate said.

"I won't be," Dicky said. "I won't be mean to you or to Ashley ever again."

Sara Kate thought about it. It would be great if she could get Dicky to promise never to be mean to anyone else in the world. But teddy bear underwear was good for only so much. Besides, she had other superpowers to keep him in line. Maybe even spelling backward would come in handy someday.

"Deal," she said. "But you'd better watch it, Dicky. Today I can tell what kind of underwear you have on. Who knows what I'll be able to do next."

"I'll watch it," Dicky said.

Sara Kate walked away from him and back to Ashley. "Dicky isn't going to be mean to us ever again," she said. "I got him to promise."

"How did you do that?" Ashley asked.

Sara Kate's arm was tingling again, much to her relief. "Someday I'll tell you," she said. "Meanwhile, just think of me as a superhero in training!"